UNSUNG:

William Moultrie and the Battle of Sullivan's Island

UNSUNG:
William Moultrie and the Battle of Sullivan's Island

NORM RICKEMAN

An Interpretive Guide

PALMETTO

PUBLISHING

Charleston, SC
www.PalmettoPublishing.com

Paperback ISBN: 9798822961234

Dedication

To my wife, Kathy Murphy, who has put up with my obsession for this project. That tolerance was challenged when I forgot our anniversary this year. When I asked her which one it was, she said "thirty-one." My response was "Hey, that's the exact number of cannons that Colonel Moultrie had on June 28, 1776." She was not amused.

Contents

Illustrations

INTRODUCTION

On June 28, 1776, British army and navy forces were re-pelled by the South Carolina militia in Charles Town Harbor. Charles Town was an economic and strategic jewel on the east coast of the colonies, not just in the south, but on the whole coast, and the British wanted to secure its control as the colonial rebellion was brewing. They also chose Charles Town as a target because it was virtually "undefended" in their view. But the best military force in the world at the time was defeated by militia led by Colonel William Moultrie from a defensive post on Sullivan's Island, a barrier island at the entrance to Charles Town Harbor. That post consisted of a palmetto-log and sand fort that had been started in January 1776 and was not yet fully completed at the time of the attack. It was manned by 435 raw militia members with 31 cannons. The British had 9 warships, over 250 cannons in the attacking fleet, and over 2,000 redcoats on the neighboring Long Island poised for attack. Moultrie had been advised by more senior military "experts" to abandon the fort on Sullivan's Island, as it was a "slaughter pen" and the British fleet would reduce it to rubble in "less than thirty minutes." Yet he held his ground, literally, and executed arguably the biggest upset victory in America's military history.

How did this happen, and why is it largely lost in our nation's history? Those are the questions I will try to answer in this book. They are the questions I asked myself in 2021 when I started as a National Park Service (NPS) volunteer at Fort Moultrie on Sullivan's Island. As a native Minnesotan and lifelong history buff, I had never heard of William Moultrie or the Battle of Sullivan's Island. I read the materials from the NPS on the subject and got a copy of the only book written on it at the time from the author himself. That book, *Victory on Sullivan's Island,* by David Lee Russell, was published in 2002 and was now out of print. NPS historian Ed Bearss had written a treatise on the battle in 1968, but it was never released for a wide audience. The battle comprises the first chapter of John Buchanan's excellent account of South Carolina's role in the revolution, *The Road to Guilford Courthouse.* C. L. Bragg has written the only modern biography of William Moultrie, *Crescent Moon over Carolina,* which was published in 2013. More recent accounts of the battle have been published, but none, in my opinion, adequately positions the events that occurred in Charles Town Harbor in 1776. All of these sources, excepting the Russell book, include events in 1780 when Charles Town did fall to the British in their second expedition to the southern theater. It is almost as if the events of 1776 in Charles Town Harbor are not worthy of examination on their own. I agree with David Russell that they are. As we approach the 250th anniversary of the Battle of Sullivan's Island, it's time to reexamine the historical significance of the battle and Moultrie himself.

This book is a history of the events that occurred but focuses more on the bigger picture than traditional military histories that emphasize details of troop movements, weaponry, and the like. Moultrie and the battle are so grossly underrepresented in American history that my intent is to get the word out in an accessible, readable, and, I hope, entertaining fashion. This work is a companion piece to my talk under the same title that I started giving around South Carolina in 2024. I think of this publication as an interpretive conversation with you, the reader. I did not do an exhaustive search of primary sources for any new insights on Moultrie or the battle. As sparse as existing secondary sources are, they are adequate for the historical details at this point. In that regard, I am indebted to the sources mentioned above, especially David Russell. I did read the eight hundred-page memoir of William Moultrie to get more insights into the events, yes, but more so the man. A list of all the relevant books and publications that I have used is included in the Sources section. I have intentionally not cluttered up the narrative with citations and footnotes. I realize this omission will upset true historians, but I want the story to flow as it would in a conversation. I do cite significant quotations and excerpts drawn from their specific sources.

Charles Town fell to the British in 1780, an event widely viewed as the biggest patriot defeat of the Revolutionary War. So why do we really care about a victory there in 1776? First, we care simply because the battle itself, and the players involved, are fascinating. I find the story has resonated with thousands of visitors to Fort Moultrie over the years and with audiences throughout South Carolina when I speak on the subject. Second, we care because it gave our brand-new nation a great confidence boost after the Declaration of Independence was signed on July 4. Declaring independence was a great leap of faith by our founding fathers, and we must not forget that the outcome at that time was in no way certain. The news of the victory over significant British military forces in Charles Town arrived in Philadelphia many days after the signing and most certainly must have strengthened our leaders' resolve. Third, we care because it prevented the British from controlling a key economic and strategic asset on the east coast for four years. The British were much more likely to have controlled the local population of the Carolinas in 1776. Tories and loyalists abounded, with many other citizens looking to maintain neutrality. I believe, in the early days of the war, the British would not have faced the same level of resistance they faced in 1780. They could have controlled the Carolinas and created a true southern front that would have challenged George Washington in the north at a very vulnerable time for the Continental Army. By 1780 the war was real, giving hope to patriotic resolve. After four frustrating years, the war-weary British enacted policies that antagonized the local Carolinian populations and drove many to the patriot cause. Patriotic defense was given valuable time to develop and proved very stout in 1780 and 1781.

Would a British victory at Sullivan's Island in 1776, then, have led to ultimate defeat for the patriots' cause? It is an intriguing question, but I am not a fan of revisionist histories. That said, I am also not a fan of ignoring the pivotal role that South Carolina played in winning our nation's independence. That contribution started in a big way on June 28, 1776.

CHAPTER 1:
SETTING THE STAGE

The Province of Carolina
and Charles Town before 1775

The states of South and North Carolina today were original-
ly encompassed by the Province of Carolina, formed by the
British in 1763. The province also consisted of all or part of the
present-day states Georgia, Florida, Alabama, Tennessee, and
Mississippi. King Charles II saw the province as a buffer to the
Spanish to the south and as a hindrance to any northern expansion on their part. The charter granted title to the land to eight
lord proprietors. These British noblemen differed greatly in their
active involvement in America, but they exercised great pow-
ers, second only to the king himself. In early 1670, they founded
a new settlement, named Charles Town after the king, on the
shore of what is today known as the Ashley River in Charles-

ton. The settlement of two hundred colonists moved in 1680 to the peninsula between the Ashley and the Cooper Rivers, where Charleston is today. The original site was mosquito ridden and lacked an ocean breeze to offset the grueling summer heat and humidity. The peninsula site was also much better defensively and offered the possibility of a viable port.

In 1674, the Grand Council of Carolina resolved to place a gun at the mouth of Charles Town Harbor. They selected an unnamed barrier island and appointed a captain in the militia to be responsible for manning a signal cannon. That man was Florence O'Sullivan. O'Sullivan was an Irishman of questionable character and prickly temperament. He had previously served as surveyor general of Carolina after convincing a lord proprietor or two that he had surveying skills, which he most certainly did not have. After this controversial posting, he now was in charge of firing the signal cannon if a Spanish, French, or pirate ship was spotted. The shot would alert the Charles Town settlement. The barrier island was later named Sullivan's Island, but no record exists as to when or why the "O" was dropped. O'Sullivan never was granted land on the island.

Historical events in the first three-quarters of the eighteenth century included the establishment in 1707 of Sullivan's Island as a major destination point of the Middle Passage slave trade. The Yamasee War of 1715 to 1717 was a very bloody conflict with indigenous people near Charles Town. In 1718, the pirate Blackbeard blockaded Charles Town Harbor for ransom. In 1721, the colonies of North and South Carolina were formed as part of the breakup of the Province of Carolina, and the lord proprietors were replaced by royal governors. As the first half of the century progressed, Charles Town boomed, with rice, indigo, the slave trade, and phosphates and other minerals driving a very diverse economy. New conflict erupted in the period 1758 to 1761 with the Cherokee Wars in South Carolina. Part of the French and Indian War, this conflict provided military experience and leadership to many individuals who will be key to our main story.

The Slave Trade

The slave trade mentioned previously deserves more attention, as the contributions of enslaved labor are also key to our story. The rough numbers of the Middle Passage are twelve million enslaved put on ships, with ten million arriving alive in the New World. Most of the enslaved were sent to South America, the West Indies, and other locations in the Caribbean. A relatively small portion, 400,000, went directly to the American colonies. Approximately half that number came through South Carolina, and the majority of those came through Sullivan's Island.

Sullivan's Island was a major hub of the Middle Passage slave trade from 1707 to 1799. It was a quarantine site. Arriving slave ships with sickness on board would have to quarantine both the enslaved and the crew. After a quarantine of at least eight days, the enslaved would enter Charles Town for auction, and the crew would be released or reassigned back to a ship. The quarantine would consist of staying shipbound off the island for milder cases, while the seriously ill were brought onshore and put in a "pest house." These wooden structures were thirty by ten feet, and four were built on the island over the years, but never more than one at the same time. Quarantine operations were switched to Morris Island at the turn of the century, thus ending Sullivan Island's role.

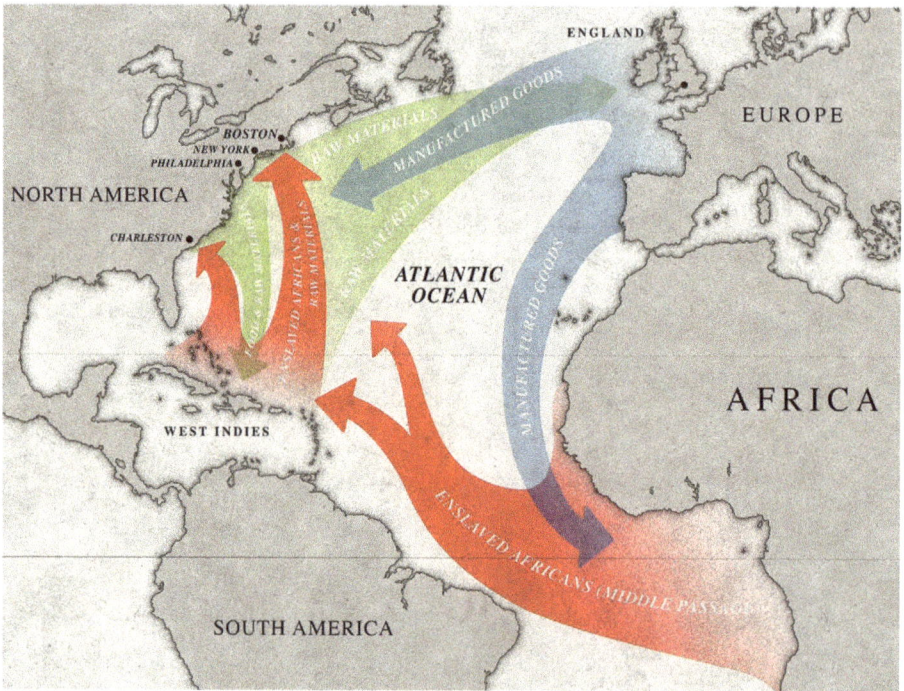

THE MIDDLE PASSAGE SLAVE TRADE
This map shows the primary movement of enslaved Africans, raw materials, and manufactured goods. The most active years of the slave trade were 1700 to 1808, when it was abolished.
Source: National Park Service

South Carolina and Charles Town in 1775

Charles Town was the fourth largest city in the colonies in 1775 but by far the richest. The list of wealthiest individuals in all the colonies was headed by Philadelphia merchant Robert Morris, but Charles Town planters dominated the top dozen spots. As mentioned earlier, the economy was very diverse and lucrative, with rice, indigo, phosphates, minerals, and the slave trade as contributors. Rice planters earned the moniker "The Rice Kings" for their wealth, prestige, and influence.

The white population of Charles Town in 1775 was approximately 12,000 with an additional 40,000 enslaved people working the plantations and fields. For South Carolina as a whole, including Charles Town, there were approximately 70,000 whites, with an additional 110,000 enslaved. Of the white population, 40,000 resided in what was called the back country and upcountry in the middle and top portion of the colony. The coastal and southern region was considered the low country.

There were considerable class rifts in the colony. Much of the population outside the low country mistrusted the Rice Kings of the south, as they felt colonial administration was focused on Charles Town, and their needs were secondary. (Back country and upcountry people were sometimes referred to as the "Pack of Beggars" by the upper classes.) South Carolinians were fiercely independent and self-reliant. Some back country settlers had grouped together in 1767 to combat a crime wave

11

there. These "regulators," as they were called, quickly became viewed by the locals as worse than the outlaws, and a second group, the "moderators," was established to control the regulators, with similarly less than desirable results.

The factional nature of this population became evident as the revolution brewed. South Carolina had participated in the 1774 Continental Congress, but a large portion of the population, especially outside the low country, were Tories, loyalists, or neutral on rebellion. Fighting in South Carolina during the American Revolution has been called America's first civil war, and that description is fitting. The first Revolutionary War bloodshed in South Carolina occurred in November of 1775, when Tories attacked Ninety Six, a stockade built by patriots. (Ninety Six got its name from traders in the early eighteenth century, as it was the estimated distance to a Cherokee trading village.) The patriots had come north to retrieve a shipment of one thousand pounds of gunpowder intended for the Cherokee that had been seized by loyalists. Casualties were light, and the loyalists disengaged after three days of siege, but this action was the first land battle of the war south of New England.

In early 1775, South Carolina proceeded to prepare militarily for revolution. A Council of Safety was formed, and it created three regiments of militia to be newly organized with ten companies each. The 1st Regiment was headed by Christopher Gadsden, the 2nd Regiment was headed by William Moultrie, and the 3rd Regiment was a unit of rangers headed by William "Danger" Thomson. Gadsden was a mer-

WILLIAM MOULTRIE
Source: American Battlefield Trust

chant and delegate to both the 1774 and 1775 Continental Congresses and held the rank of colonel in the militia. Moultrie was also a colonel in the militia and had military experience in the Cherokee Wars of 1760. He was a trusted planter who had largely married into his wealth. The third colonel, Thomson, was an indigo farmer who had also served in the Cherokee Wars. He had also led his mounted rangers in the taking and defending of Ninety Six in 1775. Thomson played a role on Sullivan's Island, as we shall see, and Moultrie will be the preeminent individual figure in our story.

Moultrie was asked by the Council of Safety to design the flag for the militia and created the flag that represents South Carolina to this day. It has indigo blue as a base and a white crescent in the upper left corner. The word *liberty* is sometimes seen in white in the crescent or across the bottom of the flag. (The palmetto tree that is on the South Carolina state flag today was added in January 1861.) Controversy exists to this day as to the crescent. While it appears to be a crescent moon, the consensus is that it was not intended as a moon. Moultrie's militia had caps that had a similar crescent insignia. That insignia represented a gorget, which was a piece of medieval armor used for neck protection. In Moultrie's original design, the crescent was placed vertically, with the points pointing up, hardly a moon symbol but consistent with the gorget argument. In 1910, the crescent was angled to its current location on the state flag. A more recent interpretation is that the crescent is the British cadency signifying a second son. As first sons inherited 100 percent of family estates, the second sons had to make it on their own, and many did that in the new world. Hence, the second son was very symbolic to many, including Moultrie, who was a second son. He served under William Bull in the Cherokee Wars and would have seen the crescent as part of the Bull family crest. Moultrie doesn't offer any clues in his memoirs, as he only refers to the symbol as a "crescent."

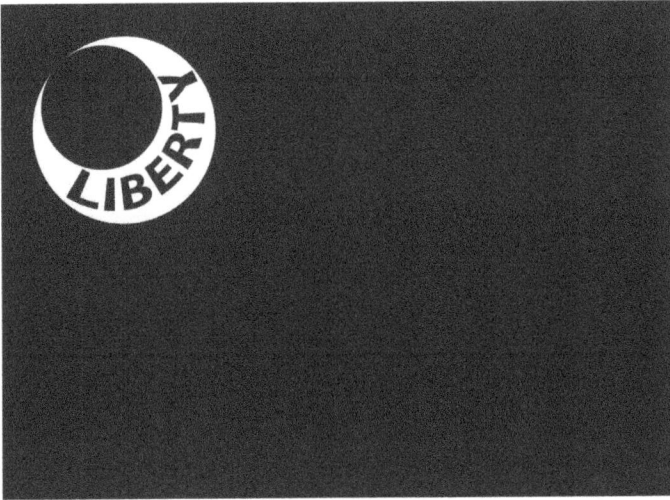

THE MOULTRIE FLAG
Source: Public Domain

As patriotic forces and flags were being created in their colonies, the royal governors of Georgia and North and South Carolina were forced to seek protection on British ships in nearby harbors. The royal governor of South Carolina, Lord William Campbell, was ousted from his quarters and was on a British ship in Charles Town Harbor. They all had the similar view that the rebellion was being fomented from New England

and was not really that popular with the southern populations. In Charles Town, Campbell had the belief that the economy was thriving, and the last thing the planters wanted to do was upset the apple cart. He and the other royal governors had known many of the planters for years. They thought of them as friends who didn't have the heart for a serious fight with Britain. Therefore, the three royal governors sent a plea to London for this remedy: send ships and troops en masse to the southern colonies, and watch this rebellion dissipate very quickly.

The British forces would be met by Tory and loyalist forces in North Carolina who would assist in controlling any patriot opposition. The British prime minister, Lord Frederick North, and the secretary of state for the colonies, Lord Dartmouth (William Legge), responded. A massive fleet of frigates, support ships, and transports was commissioned for departure at the end of 1775 from Cork, Ireland. They were to meet up with General Henry Clinton and 1,400 redcoats, sailing down from Boston, in Cape Fear Harbor, off the coast of North Carolina. The best army and navy in the world would then proceed to overpower any opposition and control the southern colonies with the support of the local loyal forces. This result, in effect, would create a permanent southern front to oppose rebellious activities in the north.

What could possibly go wrong?

CHAPTER 2:
THE FLEET AND THE FORT

The Fleet

On October 15, 1775, Lord North met with King George III to present the idea of the southern expedition. He described it as an aggressive measure that would alarm the Americans, revive the spirits of the loyalists, and be "likely to bring matters in North America to a speedy decision" (Russell, 2002, 54). The king responded the next day with approval but recommended that the expedition not exceed two thousand men and that most should be Irishmen. The king ordered four regiments to embark in the second week in December. A fifth was added, and the fleet was charged with leaving on December 12 from Cork, Ireland. These regiments were intended to become the British standing forces in the southern colonies. Yet another increase in the fleet was made on October 25 when two additional regiments were added to accompany the fleet to Cape Fear and then proceed north to reinforce General Howe in the colonies. Those forces had been dispatched earlier in the month but had been delayed by poor weather. On November 1, the total size of the fleet was targeted at 56 ships and 9,095 men.

The overall command was given to Sir Peter Parker. Parker was an Irishman. His father had been a rear admiral in the British navy. Navy service was clearly in his blood. He went to sea first with his father and then rose through the ranks, with postings primarily in the Mediterranean. He rose to fame in 1757 in the war with France, seeing combat in the West Indies. He was knighted for his service in 1772 and had attained the rank of commodore but was always seeking an opportunity to advance that rank. That opportunity seemed to have presented itself in 1775 with command of the Cape Fear expedition.

On November 7, Lord Dartmouth sent a letter to Josiah Martin, the royal governor of North Carolina, with the status of the expedition. He noted that if the entrance

SIR PETER PARKER
Source: National Park Service

18

to Cape Fear River were to be too shallow, the troops disem-
barked there could not be supported by the British warships if
the landing was opposed by patriot forces. If that were the case,
Parker had been instructed to sail south to Charles Town "in
order to try what may be effected there towards restoring Government in South Carolina." He also reminded Martin what
this entire expedition was based upon: "this enterprise is entire-
ly formed upon the assurances given by yourself and the rest of
His Majesty's Governors in the Southern Provinces, that, even
upon the appearance of a Force, much Inferior to what is now
sent, the Friends of Government would show themselves, and
the Rebellion be crushed and subdued" (Russell, 2002, 65).

As the original December date for disembarkation from
Cork approached, it was clear that the fleet was not ready. Detailed orders had not been dispatched to all commanders, the
naval convoy was not complete, and ordnance and troops were
not yet loaded. Major General Lord Charles, Earl Cornwallis,
had requested that his regiment be included in the expedition
even though he knew he would not be in command when he
arrived in America. As the top ranking army officer of the fleet,
he took control over the loading of the British troops with a
new target date of January 7 to complete that effort. Cornwallis was an aristocrat, educated at Eton and Cambridge. He had
joined the army in 1757 and seen action in the Seven Years'
War in Europe. He also was a politician, serving in both houses of Parliament in the 1760s. He had voted against the 1765
Stamp Act and was generally sympathetic to the American colonists. He had stayed active in military affairs and had been

promoted to major general in September 1775. He began his service in America with this posting.

Despite Cornwallis's efforts, continual delays due to late transport arrivals and weather problems beset the expedition. January passed. As an interesting aside, during this time, some American prisoners of war being held in Britain were assigned to the fleet for exchange in America. The most notable name was Ethan Allen. He and his New Hampshire Green Mountain Boys had gained fame when they took Fort Ticonderoga in May 1775, the first offensive victory for the patriots in the war. Colonel Benedict Arnold had been commissioned by the Massachusetts Committee on Safety to take the fort. In recruiting the Boys, he found that they refused to serve under anyone other than Ethan Allen, which compelled Arnold to accede to those wishes. British resistance was light. It was a huge victory, and Allen's reputation grew. He was captured in September 1775 in an ill-fated attack on Montreal. His impetuousness led him to attack on his own before the assault was fully coordinated and ordered. Allen was then taken to London and tried. George Washington commented on Allen's capture as a cautionary tale to officers who wanted to "outshine their generals."

LORD CORNWALLIS
Source: National Park Service

The Cape Fear Expedition finally left Cork on February 12, 1776. Included were 2,500 troops from 7 regiments under Cornwallis, 9 warships, and about 40 ordnance, supply, and transport ships. Their plan was still to meet with a British army fleet off the coast of North Carolina.

Back in October 1775, the commanding officer of the British force in the colonies, General Thomas Gage, had been called back to London to report on the war's status. Major General William Howe took over command until Gage returned. One of his first duties was to assign the officer who would meet the fleet coming from Cork and assume command of the army forces in the south. He chose his second in command, General Henry Clinton, for this duty. They were both engaged in the siege of Boston at the time. Clinton was eager to leave the mundane siege duty, and Howe was eager to let him go, finding him "thin-skinned and touchy." Clinton received his orders on January 6, 1776, and was to proceed immediately to Cape Fear, reconnoiter the landing site, and await the arrival of the fleet.

Henry Clinton was also born into an English military family, with his father an admiral and his mother the daughter of a general. His early years are historically murky, with the date and location of his birth in question, but the year 1730 is now widely accepted. The family was definitely connected, and Henry had gone to the Americas the first time in 1743, when his father was the governor of the Province of New York. In 1749, he had returned to England to pursue his military career. He had served in the Seven Years' War and was promoted to major-general in 1772. He obtained a seat in Parliament that same year and was a member until 1784. He returned to America in 1775 and fought at Bunker Hill. He set sail from Boston in January 1776 with a small fleet and 1,500 men to meet the larger fleet coming from Cork. He stopped in New York and Hampton Roads, Virginia, before leaving on the last leg to Cape Fear in late March. He arrived well in advance of Parker's fleet and experienced frustration in the waiting. While all this was going on, things had heated up in inland North Carolina.

On February 27, 1776, the much-touted (by the royal governors at least) loyalist forces who had risen up to meet the British fleet met a patriot army at Moores Creek Bridge, about fifty miles inland. In a few minutes, it was over. The loyalist forces had started their march to the coast with 1,600 men but lost many to attrition. At the time of the battle, they numbered about 800 to 900 and were faced by a like number of patriots. The patriots had 2 casualties (1 dead), while the loyalists had 50 casualties and 850 captured. It was a major patriot victory. A statement had been made about the real fighting vigor of the loyalists and the perceived timidity of the patriotic response. The Battle of Moores

GENERAL
HENRY CLINTON
Source:
National Park Service

Creek Bridge is classified as a "minor" engagement in the Revolutionary War. Yet it accomplished two great things. First, it protected North Carolina from a British invasion. Second, it forced the British fleet to choose their Plan B—go to Charles Town and secure South Carolina.

Peter Parker's fleet finally made it to Cape Fear in April and consolidated with Clinton's forces. After a lengthy stay for discussion of all the strategic options and rest and refitting, the assault portion of the force left for Charles Town on May 31. Their intelligence had told them, in Cornwallis's words, that Charles Town was virtually "undefended." The best army and navy in the world were now poised to attack this undefended jewel of a target.

What could possibly go wrong?

BATTLE OF MOORES CREEK BRIDGE
Source: National Park Service (wayside exhibit at battle site)

The Fort

The defense of Charles Town Harbor at the end of 1775 consisted of Fort Johnson on James Island, which had been abandoned by the British under patriot pressure. William Moultrie was stationed there after the British left in September, and that was why he was asked to create the militia flag. The Moultrie flag was first flown at Fort Johnson and signaled that it was now in patriot hands. (Fort Johnson would fire the first shot of the American Civil War eighty-five years later when its mortar round exploded over Fort Sumter. That shot was the signal for other batteries to open fire.) A second line of defense was at Haddrell's Point (present-day Mount Pleasant), where batteries were installed in December. The 1776 map of Charles Town Harbor below shows these locations, plus the strategic nature of the harbor for both economic and military purposes.

The entrance to the harbor was protected by sandbars, and the inner harbor was likewise rife with sand. Two barrier islands, Sullivan's Island and Long Island (present-day Isle of Palms) were also at or near the harbor entrance. These islands are separated by a waterway called Breach Inlet, which will later play a major part in our story.

In January, South Carolina colonial governor John Rutledge and the Council of Safety recommended that another defensive position be established on Sullivan's Island. It was ideally suited at the mouth of the harbor, and the deep water required for large ships would take any invading fleet well within cannon range. A fortification on the southwestern end of a two-and-a-

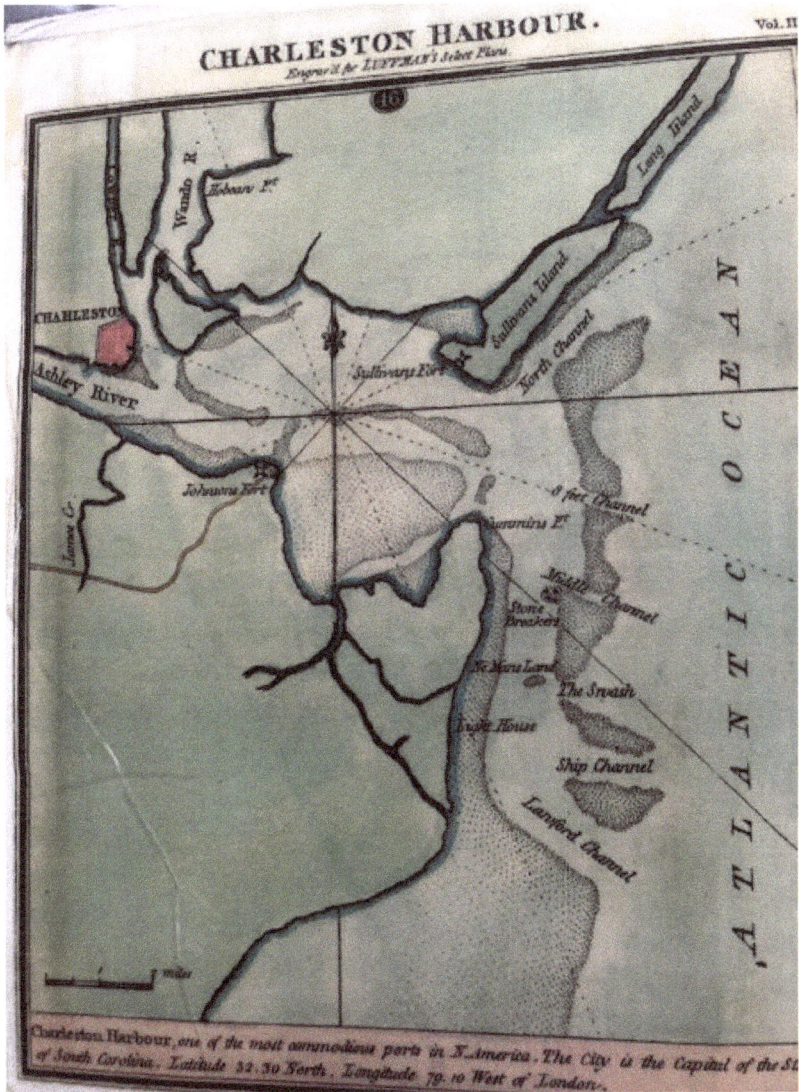

1776 CHARLES TOWN HARBOR MAP
Note how the sandbars and shoals force any invading naval fleet to use the deep water near Sullivan's Island, well within cannon range.
Source: National Park Service (The author uses this placard to show visitors to Fort Moultrie why the fort on Sullivan's Island was in such a good strategic position.)

half-mile beach was authorized. It was targeted at twenty feet in height and was to be made from mud and sand held in place by walls of palmetto logs. The location of the fort was largely a swamp, with myrtle and palmetto trees and some live oak. Palmetto trees were chosen as the building material because of their nearby abundance. While hard to the touch, they are spongy and porous on the inside. Botanists do not technically classify them as trees because they don't have a solid trunk. The procurement of the logs was contracted out, as was the construction, where enslaved labor played the key role. Moultrie was charged with providing one hundred militia men to protect the site.

On March 1, 1776, Moultrie was officially ordered to take command of Sullivan's Island and oversee completion of the fort. He described the site this way in his memoirs: "It was quite a wilderness, and a thick swamp, where the fort stands, covered with live oak, myrtle and palmetto trees" (Moultrie, 1802, vol. 1, 122). Two twenty-foot palmetto log walls were constructed in parallel, bound together with timber, and then the space between filled with sixteen feet of sand and dirt. (As an aside, also in March, South Carolina declared itself independent of England and appointed John Rutledge as its first president of a separate nation.)

The fort on Sullivan's Island was intended to hold up to 1,000 men. Moultrie had 435 men and 31 cannon when the British made their assault. The fort was not complete at the time of the attack, with the back walls unfinished and vulnerable to attack.

THE FORT ON SULLIVAN'S ISLAND
Note the unfinished portion in the rear.
Source: National Park Service

In early June, the British fleet appeared off near-by Dewees Island and soon offloaded the army forces onto Long Island, where they established an encampment. The navy would later proceed to the mouth of the harbor, where they would undertake the laborious task of crossing the Charles Town Harbor bar. This effort required them to offload the heavy guns onto smaller ships to lighten a frigate's load. They then reloaded the guns onto the ships. They would regroup at the deep water of Five Fathom Hole off Morris Island and prepare for attack. The land forces on Long Island would then execute a battle plan coordinated with that naval attack. They would cross the water barrier between Long Island and Sullivan's Island, Breach Inlet, at low tide, when water depth was predicted to be 1.5 feet. Over two thousand redcoats would simply march across and overcome the patriot defenses at Breach Inlet. Those formidable defenses, led by Col. Danger Thomson, totaled 780 militia and two cannon.

At this same time, Sullivan's Island received an esteemed, controversial, and, later, ignominious visitor. Charles Lee was a British military man who had served in the Seven Years' War on American soil and later returned to Europe, sold his commission, and served with the Polish army. He came to America in 1773 and was a landowner in Virginia. In 1775, he volunteered to serve with the patriot forces. His reputation was such that he was considered for commander in chief of the Continental Army (and he lobbied for the role), but George Washington was named, and Lee served under him. With the British fleet approaching Charles Town, Washington appointed Lee to command of the southern theater. (Lee sent Continental forces from North Carolina and Virginia to shore up Charles Town defenses, but these forces were not engaged during the coming battle.)

The South Carolina militias were attached to the Continental Army in November 1775. However, the chain of command was loose, to say the least. Moultrie reported to, and took his lead from, the Council on Safety and his childhood friend John Rutledge. When Lee arrived on June 7 to oversee the coming action, he set about revising gun placements and had strong opinions about the defensibility of the fort

GENERAL CHARLES LEE
Source: National Park Service (the second image is
included as a caricature better befitting his personality)

on Sullivan's Island. Moultrie's first impression was extremely positive. He stated initially in his memoirs that Lee was
"worth a thousand men" (Moultrie, 1802, vol. 1, 141). That
opinion quickly changed. Lee strongly advised President
Rutledge to abandon the post, as it was a "slaughter pen"
(Moultrie, 1802, vol. 1, 141). Rutledge then told Moultrie,
"General Lee wishes you to evacuate the fort. You will not
without an order from me. I will sooner cut off my hand than
write one." (Moultrie, 1802, vol. 1, 141; exact quote from
National Park Service).

Moultrie told Lee he thought he could defend the post, upon which Lee insisted on an escape route. A bridge was to be constructed to the mainland for that purpose. Lee also insisted that a traverse be built inside the fort as a secondary defensive position. Moultrie gave lip service to these tasks and later said that he never considered retreat and defeat as options. A sea captain named Lamperer visited the fort as the British fleet neared, and this exchange (with author's comments in parentheses) took place: (Moultrie, 2002, vol. 1, 143-4)

Lamperer: "well Colonel, what do you think of it now" (referring to the imposing enemy fleet)

Moultrie: "we should beat them"

Lamperer: "Sir, when those ships (pointing to the men-of-war) come to lay alongside of your fort, they will knock it down in half an hour."

Moultrie: "we will lay behind the ruins and prevent them from landing."

Moultrie's calm confidence is apparent in this exchange.

Charles Lee was a classic martinet, and his frustration grew. The bridge, made of boats and timber tied together, proved unworkable, and the traverse was slow in construction. He was also frustrated that the back of the fort was exposed and thought Moultrie should have been harder on his men and the enslaved labor to get everything done. He continued to press for evacuation. In his fine book, *Victory on Sullivan's Island*, David Russell includes a passage that is very telling on the command structure and Moultrie himself. Russell records these events that took place on June 23 and 24):

> In the afternoon, John Rutledge met William Moultrie on Broad Street at the steps to Dillon's Tavern as Moultrie headed to drink down a julep, his favorite, and distinctly Southern drink. After their greetings, Moultrie told Rutledge that having been warned three times about completing a bridge from Haddrell's Point to Sullivan's Island, Lee had ordered him to evacuate the fort. As a point of honor and as a show of defiant authority, Rutledge told Moultrie to go back to Fort Sullivan immediately and stay there. Rutledge asked his old friend to whom did he owe allegiance. With a slight delay Moultrie responded "To General Lee." The President asked how he knew that, which Moultrie replied that he himself had given Lee the command authority over the militia. Moultrie admitted that he had not personally seen the proclamation. Rutledge asked whether he had a habit of accepting military orders from his superior officer except in writing or in person. Moultrie indicated no. Rutledge then told Moultrie to obey him (Lee) in everything, except in leaving Fort Sullivan: " do nothing openly to destroy moral."

Colonel Moultrie returned to the fort and took a nap under the uncompleted bastion where the shade was best toward the west. The next day Lee returned to Sullivan's Island by canoe and found Moultrie under a shade tree with a julep in his hand. Quickly, but with some difficulty owing to his gout, the colonel stood up and saluted Lee. Lee asked why he had disobeyed his order to leave the island. Moultrie made up an excuse that he was having a hard time obtaining boats. Clearly frustrated, Lee made a rapid inspection and went off as he repeated his orders to Moultrie to "move to the mainland, and leave only a skeleton force for vidette duty." Lee's frustration would only increase as each day passed (2002, 198–9).

On June 27, Lee decided to relieve Moultrie of command. His replacement was to be a Colonel Nash from the North Carolina Continentals then stationed at Haddrell's Point. He told Nash that Moultrie was a "half-baked country militiaman" and to meet him (Lee) the next day to assume command.

Despite several delays due to weather, logistics, and coordination issues, the morning of June 28, 1776, saw the world's best army and navy now poised to attack. Charles Town's defense was an unfinished log and sand fort, built by slaves and manned by 435 untested militia troops. Additional raw militia, 780 strong, were stationed at Breach Inlet under Danger Thomson, but with only two cannon. The leadership structure was in flux, and the man still in charge was a gout-ridden, "half-baked country militiaman."

Oh what, what could possibly go wrong?

CHAPTER 3:
JUNE 28, 1776

Henry Clinton had grown increasingly frustrated with Commodore Parker's challenges in initiating the attack. Clinton had also discovered ten days earlier that his own assault was going to be more difficult. The low tide assurances of 1.5 feet at Breach Inlet proved to be false, as low tide was 7 feet at the time. He sought alternative assault options, but none were ideal, and none afforded the option of adequate support by a British frigate. He did have fifteen flatboats that could transport a total of four hundred men at a time, but without naval support. Danger Thomson's defenders were in a very strong position.

Another attempt to initiate the naval attack by Parker failed on Thursday, June 27, when the wind shifted and forced the fleet to stop. But the next day, the weather was favorable, and it began. Troop dispositions on the morning of June 28 are shown on the following page.

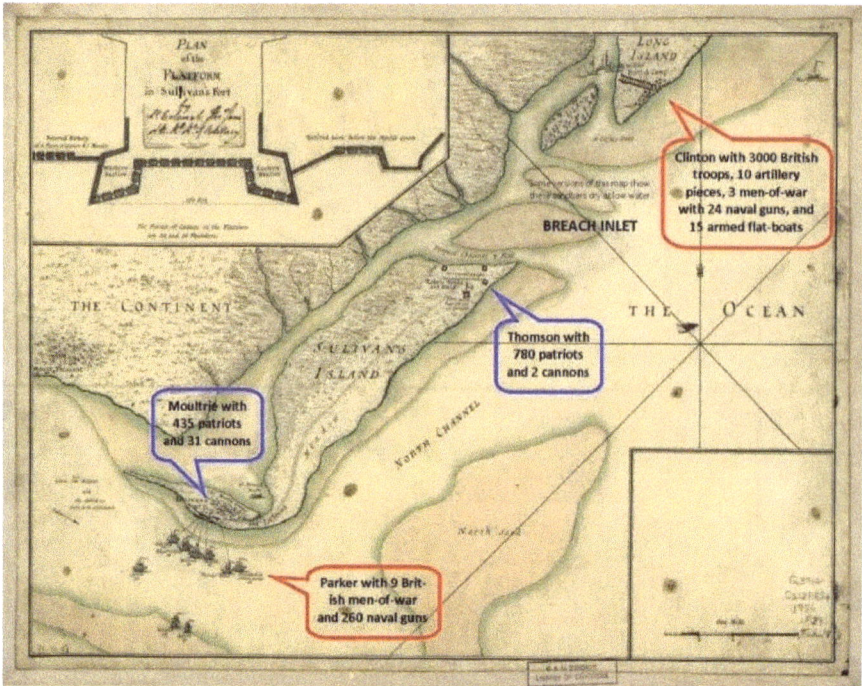

APPROXIMATE FORCE DISPOSITIONS ON JULY 28, 1776
Source: Library of Congress (from RevolutionaryWar.us website)

At 9:00 a.m., Parker claimed to have ordered that a signal be sent to Clinton that the assault was on. Clinton later claimed that he never got it. Communication and coordination between the two leaders would not be stellar this day. At the same time, Colonel Moultrie was riding with Danger Thomson reviewing an advanced guard post between the fort and Breach Inlet. They saw the British ships loosen their topsails and hurriedly returned to their respective posts, as they knew the attack was underway.

At 10:20 a.m., the patriots opened fire on the fifty-gun *Bristol*, Parker's flagship, and the twenty-eight gun *Active*. The *Bristol* and the fifty-gun *Experiment* were the first British ships to return fire. The British bomb ship, the *Thunder*, fired an early mortar round that landed dangerously close to the fort's magazine, which had been tucked in the far rear. No damage was done. The twenty-two-gun *Friendship* and the twenty-eight-gun *Solebay* rounded out the first wave of the naval assault. The second wave was made up of the twenty-gun *Sphinx*, the twenty-eight gun *Actaeon*, and the twenty-eight gun *Siren*. These three ships were trying to make an end run and get behind the fort to take advantage of the unfinished barricades there. In his memoirs, Moultrie concedes that had this maneuver been successful, the fort would likely have fallen. However, all three ships ran aground on the sand shoal (near present-day Fort Sumter). The *Siren* and *Sphinx* were able to extract themselves, but not without damage. The *Actaeon* was trapped. The end run had failed.

The British pounded the fort with over 250 cannon. Moultrie responded with 25 of his own, as the other 6 were positioned for inland attack. The British ships were not able to get as close to the walls of the land fortification as successful tactics would have required. The *Bristol* and other lead ships were steered by black pilots who were renowned for their knowledge of the treacherous harbor. The sand kept them three hundred to four hundred yards away from the palmetto log fort. The painting below of the naval assault is very impressive but also very misleading in that regard. If the British ships had gotten as close as the painting suggests, it is likely the patriot cannoneers would have been in serious peril and the walls would likely have succumbed to the close-in barrage (as Captain Lampere had warned Moultrie). It has been posed in recent years that perhaps the black pilots intentionally held back to support the patriot cause. That scenario is extremely unlikely, as the enslaved were no friends to the patriots. In fact, the British had offered freedom to any enslaved male who could escape to fight for the Crown.

BATTLE OF SULLIVAN'S ISLAND #1
Source: National Park Service
(currently in lobby of Fort Moultrie's Visitor Center)

The next painting is perhaps less exciting but much more accurate. It was painted after the action by Henry Grey, a wounded veteran of the battle.

BATTLE OF SULLIVAN'S ISLAND #2
The Unsuccessful Attack on the Fort on Sullivan's Island,
June 28, 1776.
Painting by Henry Grey shortly after the battle. Image courtesy
of the Gibbes Museum of Art/Carolina Art Association

FRANCIS MARION
Source: National Park Service

Moultrie had a very careful plan for firing his cannon in a methodical and economic manner. Four guns would fire at once at selected targets. Moultrie's second in command, Francis Marion, was credited by Moultrie in his memoirs as being largely responsible for accurate firing. The British also admired the patriot artillery prowess after the battle. (Marion would later become famous as the "Swamp Fox" for his guerrilla warfare successes in 1780–81.)

Charles Lee had been thwarted in his attempt to reach the island in the morning and relieve Moultrie of command, as the start of the battle precluded any such act. He did come to Sullivan's Island later as the firing was heavy, helped position some guns, and then left after about fifteen minutes with this comment to Moultrie, "Colonel, I see you are doing very well here, you have no occasion for me, I will go up to town again." (Russell, 2002, 210) The next painting depicts an officers' meeting in the interior of the fort during the battle.

BATTLE OF SULLIVAN'S ISLAND #3
The Battle of Fort Moultrie
Painting by John Blake White (1826)
Source: U.S. Senate Collection

The British had a roughly seven-to-one advantage in fire-power. Why did it seem to be going so well with those odds? The palmetto log walls of the fort turned out to be a perfect defense material. As referenced earlier, palmetto trees don't have solid trunks. The logs are very hard, but they flex and do not shatter. British cannonballs striking the walls would bounce off or even embed. Many balls flew over the walls and ended up in the swampy section in the back half of the fort. Was it fate that the only material in quantity to construct the fort in short order was also the perfect choice?

Back on Long Island, Clinton heard the naval attack and immediately began his own assault by 2,200 redcoats. His flotilla of longboats was quickly repulsed by Danger Thomson's men and grapeshot from his two cannons. They could only attack in piecemeal fashion, 400 at a time, and Clinton wisely realized such attack was futile. It would be up to the naval assault alone to win the day. Clinton was criticized by London afterward for being on the island nineteen days and not having a viable attack plan or enough boats to make the crossing. Was it fate that this usually organized and highly competent officer failed in this way? In my opinion, the British assault was not characterized by incompetence, but more by an extreme over-confidence in the inevitable result of proven arms subduing a rag-tag defense.

Back at the fort, the firing had been heaviest around mid-day. At that time, the militia flagstaff flying the Moultrie flag had been shot in half by a British cannonball. Sergeant William Jasper leaped over the ramparts and walked the length of the fort under fire. He returned the colors inside, attached them to another pole, and held the flag aloft. It was a great inspiration to the men and signaled to Charles Town that the fort was still standing.

WILLIAM JASPER
Source: National Park Service

By 3:00 p.m., the firing from the fort was stopped for an hour to preserve ammunition. It restarted at 4:00 p.m. The intervals between firings were slowly paced, and the British, many times, thought the fort had succumbed only to be rocked back to reality when the next rounds were fired. At about 7:00 p.m., the British were firing only after the patriots fired first. By 9:00 p.m., it was over. The British ships departed the way they had come, much worse for the wear. The patriot defenders had lost 12 killed and 25 wounded that day. An additional 5 of the wounded eventually succumbed to their wounds. The British ships experienced 105 killed and over 200 total casualties. Peter Campbell, the royal governor of South Carolina, was on the *Bristol* and experienced wounds, complications of which contributed to his death two years later. Another of the wounded was Sir Peter Parker himself. A ball burst near where he was standing on the *Bristol*. The force of the blast shredded his pants in the front and removed them in the back. Sir Peter Parker had been depanted. Fate?

The next morning, all the British ships were salvaged except for the *Actaeon*, which remained on the shoal. Moultrie had this observation:

Early in the morning was presented to our view, the Acteon frigate, hard, and fast aground; at about 400 yards distance: we gave her a few shot, which she returned, but they soon set fire to her, and quitted her: Capt. Jacob Milligan and others, went in some of our boats, boarded her while she was on fire, and pointed 2 or 3 guns at the Commodore, and fired them; then brought off the ships bell, and other articles, and had scarcely left her, when she blew up, and from the explosion issued a grand pillar of smoke, which soon expanded itself at the top, and to appearance, formed the figure of a palmetto tree; the ship immediately burst into a great blaze that continued till she burnt down to the water's edge (Moultrie, 1802, vol. 1, 180).

A grand pillar of smoke in the shape of a palmetto tree. Fate?

CHAPTER 4:
THE AFTERMATH

The morning of June 29 saw Charles Town awaken to no immediate danger. It was widely held that the victory was divinely ordained. There could be no other explanation for it. Reverend Oliver Hart stated, "God appeared for us, and defeated our enemies," and William Drayton praised "that Almighty Power, in whose hands, are the destinies of nations" (Russell, 2002, 220). Moultrie's casualties were deemed remarkably light, given the ferocity of the British bombardment. The patriots expended under five thousand pounds of gunpowder to the British's thirty-four thousand. Seven thousand British cannonballs were recovered from in front of the walls, inside the fort's swampy ground, and in the general vicinity of the fort.

The carnage inside the naval fleet was another story. Charles Lee's description of Moultrie's fort as a likely "slaughter pen" proved to be more apt to the actual devastation on the British ships. A British officer on the flagship *Bristol* later wrote, "During action no slaughterhouse could present so bad a sight with Bristol blood and entrails lying about" (Russell, 2002, vol. 1, 222). Moultrie had fired chain shot at the masts and grape shot at the crew, wreaking havoc. The *Bristol* had lost 64 killed and 161 wounded. The *Experiment* was second hardest hit, with 57 dead and 30 wounded, including the captain, who lost an arm.

Accolades came pouring in to Moultrie and the defenders. Although Charles Lee would count this victory on his command biography, he was effusive in his praise for Moultrie and his men to Rutledge: "Their conduct is such that as does them the greatest honor, no men ever did, and it is impossible ever can behave better" (Moultrie, 1802, vol. 1, 170). Lee also shared this sentiment with the president of the Virginia Convention and said he "had no idea that so much coolness and intrepidity could be displayed by a collection of raw recruits, as I was witness of in this garrison" (Russell, 2002, 225). His view and that of others was that if Moultrie had not had to manage his limited ammunition supply, the damage to the fleet would have been even worse, and he may have destroyed it. Moultrie had this somewhat sarcastic comment about his time with Lee: "Gen. Lee, I was informed, did not like my having the command of that important post, he did not doubt my courage but said I was too easy in command as his letters shew; but after the 28th June he made me his bosom friend " (Moultrie, 1802, vol. 1, 144). British reports of the previous day's events also praised the defenders, at the same time sending a dose of reality into their understanding of the patriots' willingness and ability to defend their land and fight for liberty. That message had also been sent at Bunker Hill the year before, but this time, it was in victory and not defeat.

On July 4, President Rutledge visited the fort for a formal victory ceremony. Moultrie was promoted to brigadier general, and the fort was officially named Fort Moultrie. Sergeant Jasper was also formally recognized for his bravery. July 4, of course, was also the day the Declaration of Independence was signed in Philadelphia. It would be an appealing image today to think that any hesitant signers, with ink pen cautiously held over the page, would have seen the doors burst open with the exciting news about the Charles Town victory, thereby giving them their final resolve. But alas, news of the victory did not reach Philadelphia until over a week later, and, of course, the resolution of the signers was never in doubt. However, this significant underdog victory against the full arms of the British Empire had to be a huge confidence boost to our new republic in the early days. The establishment of a southern force by the British had been thwarted, giving Washington and the Continental Army freedom from dealing with a southern front in the early days of the war.

The legacy of William Moultrie and this battle are shockingly underrepresented in our nation's history. That legacy will be explored later, along with possible rationale for this historical oversight. Before moving there, let's look at what became of the key places and people from our story.

Charles Town

Charles Town was safely in patriot hands until the second British invasion of the south in 1780. This time, the British wisely landed ground forces near present-day Kiawah Island in addition to attacking the harbor. The British forces crossed James and Johns Islands and laid siege to Charles Town from the north. In May 1780, Charleston surrendered, and British forces controlled the city until December 1782. The Continental Army commander defending Charles Town was Benjamin Lincoln, with Moultrie as one of his generals. (Lincoln would later be involved in another surrender. He was the officer who received the sword from the British at Yorktown in 1783. General Cornwallis refused to surrender the sword himself, instead making his subordinate do it. Washington followed suit and gave Lincoln the honor.) Lincoln, Moultrie, and the other officers were not imprisoned but paroled, meaning they had quite free rein but could not travel without permission and could not take up arms against the British. After fierce fighting in South Carolina in 1780–81, the Continental Army, led by General Nathanael Greene, finally entered Charles Town in December 1782. Fighting had largely ceased, but the war wasn't officially over until the Treaty of Paris in 1783. The name of the city was changed to Charleston after the war was officially over.

Sullivan's Island

The quarantine operations on the island for the enslaved people from West Africa moved to Morris Island in 1799. Sullivan's Island saw a settlement called Moultrieville established, and it continued to be a beach destination for the Charleston area. It supported a US Army base from the 1776 battle until 1947. Much of the island was devoted to military affairs until that time. Today it is a thriving and desirable beach community.

Fort Moultrie

After the British captured Charles Town and the harbor in 1780, Fort Moultrie was renamed Fort Arbuthnot after the admiral of the British fleet that participated in the invasion. The fort was renamed for Moultrie after the treaty in 1783. It was renamed briefly Fort Getty in the early 1900s but soon reverted back to Moultrie. As previously stated, it was an operational army base from 1776 to 1947. Many future Civil War generals served there, including William Tecumseh Sherman, John Reynolds, Braxton Bragg, and George Thomas. It was also home to Edgar Allan Poe for almost a year. Three of his stories were inspired by his time serving on Sullivan's Island. The Seminole war chief Osceola was imprisoned and died there in early 1838. Major Robert Anderson led the army base in late 1860 and in December of that year relocated his force to the new Fort Sumter in Charleston Harbor. Fort Moultrie was then occupied by southern forces and was one of several locations that fired upon Sumter the next April. In 1863, the Union made a concerted effort to retake the harbor and Charleston, but those assaults were rebuffed, despite major damage to Forts Sumter and Moultrie. Charleston fell to the Union in February 1865. The Civil War marked the end of hot military action at Moultrie, although the fort was on high alert many times, including during the Spanish-American War. Fort Moultrie was used as a command site during World War II, monitoring all harbor traffic and German U-Boat activity. It was decommissioned in 1947. Today Fort Moultrie is part of the National Park System, whose rangers and volunteers are eager to share the incredible history of this unique place with visitors.

FORT MOULTRIE
VISITOR CENTER
Source: Photo taken
by author.

Sir Peter Parker

Despite losing his pants, Sir Peter had shown remarkable courage on the deck of the battered *Bristol*. He refused to leave that deck despite pleadings from his men to do so. After he left for New York, he served under General Howe in the invasion and capture of New York City. He commanded the squadron that captured (the other) Long Island in August 1776. He was promoted to admiral in 1777, and history records him as a mentor and friend of Horatio Nelson. He continued to serve in Parliament and was made admiral of the fleet in 1799. He died in 1811.

Henry Clinton

Clinton also left for New York after the battle and played a key role in the Battle of Long Island. He and Howe soon were at odds, as Howe found Clinton somewhat annoying. He tried to get the command that went to John Burgoyne (who later was defeated at Saratoga) but was passed over. He threatened to resign but was mollified by a knighthood in 1777. After the disaster at Saratoga, Howe resigned, and Clinton was named commander-in-chief in America, a position he held until 1782. In 1780, he returned to Charles Town and participated in the siege and taking of the city. While a competent military man, he had the tendency to blame others for defeats and setbacks. He blamed Parker for the many delays in launching the attack on Sullivan's Island and for his ships' failure to get close enough to the walls of the fort to do real damage. (In 1780, it is said he went to the fort, tested the water depth for himself, and concluded that Parker could have gotten much closer.) He later would blame Lord Cornwallis for not advancing up the Carolinas fast enough in 1780–81. Clinton returned to England in 1782 and resumed his parliamentary career. He died in 1795.

General Cornwallis

Cornwallis went to New York with Clinton after the Battle of Sullivan's Island. He fought many times against George Washington in the northern theater over the next few years. As the war in the north stalemated, he returned with Clinton in 1780 as part of the successful second assault on Charles Town. 1780 and 1781 saw him and the British forces grow increasingly frustrated as they tried to control the countryside and move up through the Carolinas. Major victories like Camden were offset by major losses like Kings Mountain and Cowpens. The patriot militia and Nathanael Greene's Continental Army would not relent. Cornwallis finally abandoned the Carolinas and made his way to Virginia and his destiny at Yorktown. His surrender on October 17, 1781, marked the end of hostile action, although the Treaty of Paris didn't come until 1783. After the war, he was well received in England despite the surrender and served in leadership posts in India and Ireland. He died in 1805 in India.

William "Danger" Thomson

After the Battle of Sullivan's Island, Thomson served in the Battle of Savannah (1779) and in the 1780 defense of Charles Town. When Charles Town fell, he was taken prisoner but eventually exchanged in time to advise Nathanael Greene in his South Carolina campaign. He was promoted to brevet general in 1783. The British had occupied and devastated his plantation in South Carolina, and despite poor health exacerbated by captivity, Thomson labored to restore his indigo production after the war. When that market waned, he became a pioneer in the production of cotton for export. He died in 1796 and is buried in the Thomson family cemetery in Fort Motte, South Carolina.

Thomson got his moniker "Danger" as an indication of respect from his men for his fierceness and conduct as a fighter and leader. He received a commendation for his service on Sullivan's Island from the Continental Congress and responded to John Hancock: "my life and future are devoted to the Cause of the thirteen United States of America & to the general propagation of Liberty."

Charles Lee

Lee was recalled north, and "the hero of Charles Town" rejoined Washington in New York. It didn't take him long to criticize Washington's actions. It is said he was captured by the British in December 1776 while in a tavern writing a letter to Horatio Gates complaining about Washington's short-comings. He was taken to London but released in a prisoner exchange in April 1778. He met with Washington at Valley Forge, and his earlier opinion of him had not changed. He lobbied and jockeyed for power. While serving with Washington at Monmouth Court House, he displayed erratic behavior and was stung by Washington's criticism of him for what Lee thought was a strategic retreat. He demanded a court-martial, and Washington obliged. Lee was found guilty and suspended from the army for a year. From his estate in Virginia, he continued to complain about Washington, making himself a pest to Congress. He was terminated from service in 1780 and died from fever in 1782 in Philadelphia. His legacy is extremely mixed because of his perceived dual loyalties and prickly demeanor. He was quick to blame and criticize others, so he was widely disliked. These qualities may have sullied his reputation somewhat unfairly.

William Jasper

Sergeant Jasper's heroism in the Battle of Sullivan's Island was recognized by President Rutledge, who presented him with a sword at the July 4 victory celebration. He also offered Jasper a lieutenant's commission. Jasper turned it down, saying he was not qualified, as he could neither read nor write. After the battle, Moultrie offered Jasper a "roving commission" and a few men to "rove" the countryside, scout the enemy, and capture its men and materiel whenever possible. If captured, he would present himself as a deserter and then act as a spy for the patriots. He later joined the Siege of Savannah and was killed in October 1779. Fittingly, he died holding the standard of his regiment. Today there are multiple landmarks named for Jasper. Jasper Boulevard is a major throughway across Sullivan's Island that connects to the bridge to Isle of Palms (formerly Long Island). In 1897–98, a major battery was constructed at Fort Moultrie and named Battery Jasper in his honor. It contained large artillery on "disappearing carriages" and is part of the National Park today.

BATTERY JASPER
Source: Photo by author

Francis Marion

In many ways, the most intriguing supporting cast member has been saved for last. After Sullivan's Island, Francis Marion continued his military service with Moultrie and was given command of Fort Moultrie for a period in 1778. When Charles Town surrendered in 1780, Marion was not in the surrender zone. He had hurt his ankle and was at his plantation. Benjamin Lincoln had directed that anyone injured or otherwise unfit for duty should leave the city. He was free to continue fighting, and fight he did. His attempt to join Horatio Gates before the Battle of Camden in 1780 was thwarted when Gates sent him back toward Georgetown, South Carolina, to prevent the British from escaping to the coast. Gates had contempt for the militia. The irony was that Gates did the escaping after the fiasco that was Camden. He fled the battle early and was ridiculed for retreating nonstop on horseback for 180 miles. With the Continental Army largely gone after Camden, militia leaders like Marion, Thomas Sumter, and Andrew Pickens emerged as the only barrier to the expansion of British control north of Charles Town.

Marion was involved in twelve major battles and skirmishes in 1780–81. Marion and his men were fluid in number and frustrated the British, who tried and failed to find him. His main base camp was on Snow's Island in Florence County, South Carolina. At one point in late 1780, the British sent the dashing and controversial Colonel Banastre Tarleton to end the Marion threat. After pursuing Marion for over twen-

ty-five miles through a swamp, Tarleton was quoted as saying, "As for this old fox, the Devil himself could not catch
him." At that point, the legend known as the Swamp Fox was
born. (Ironically, Tarleton's failed attempts at defeating Marion actually started in 1776, as Tarleton was on Long Island
as part of the army forces at the Battle of Sullivan's Island.)
After Nathanael Greene took over command of the southern
campaign for the Continental Army, the militia efforts were
better aligned with the regular army. Greene had skeptical
attitudes about the capability and reliability of the militia, but
he understood how they needed to work together. He actually
emulated the hit-and-run tactics of the militias, as all four
of his major engagements in the southern theater (Guilford
Court House, Ninety Six, Hobkirk Hill, and Eutaw Springs)
were technically defeats, as the British held the fields afterward. However, British casualties and expended ammunition
were such that their force became more and more depleted.
Greene lost the battles but won the war. Marion served with
Greene in command of a line unit at Eutaw Springs, but his
guerrilla efforts earned the real praise, as Greene wrote him
in April 1781:

> When I consider how much you have done and suf-
> fered, and under what difficulties you have maintained
> your ground, I am at a loss which to admire most, your
> courage and fortitude or your address and manage-
> ment. Certain it is, no man has a better claim to the
> public thanks than you have. History affords no instance
> wherein an officer has kept possession of a country un-

der so many disadvantages as you have. Surrounded on every side by superior forces, hunted from every quarter with veteran troops, you have found means to elude their attacks, and to keep alive the expiring hopes of an oppressed militia, when all succor seemed to be cut off. To fight the enemy bravely with prospect of victory, is nothing; but to fight with intrepidity under the constant impression of defeat, and inspire irregular troops to do it, is a talent peculiar to yourself. Nothing will give me greater pleasure than to do justice to your merit, and I shall miss no opportunity of declaring to Congress, to the commander in chief of the American army, and to the world, the sense I have of your merit and your services (Boddie, 2000, 202).

After the war, Marion went back to plantation life and also served in the South Carolina Senate. A bill came up there to offer immunity to militia leaders whose men had done damage to citizens' personal property. Marion famously remarked in opposition that had his men done anything so egregious, he should, and would, be held accountable. He died in 1795 and is buried in Belle Isle Plantation Cemetery in Pineville, South Carolina.

His legacy includes more than fifty sites across the United States named in his honor. He was admitted to the US Army Ranger Hall of Fame in 1993. Like William Moultrie, Marion is underrepresented in American history for the role he played in the revolution. That said, unlike Moultrie, Marion was given national prominence in 1960 when Walt Disney ran a Swamp Fox series on his NBC show *The Wonderful World of Disney*. While it may not have had the same national buzz as his previous series on Davy Crockett, *The Swamp Fox* also featured a distinctive hat and a very catchy theme song. It starred Leslie Nielsen (before his *Airplane!* and *The Naked Gun* fame), and all episodes are available on YouTube.

FRANCIS MARION
GRAVESITE
Belle Isle Plantation Cemetery,
Pineville, SC
Source: Photo by author

MOULTRIE IN BATTLE
Source: National Park Service

CHAPTER 5:
WILLIAM MOULTRIE

The central character of our story has been William Moultrie. Hopefully, the recounting of the Battle of Sullivan's Island gives you some sense of the man. But who was William Moultrie really?

His basic biography is as follows:

William Moultrie was born on November 23, 1730, in Charles Town, South Carolina. His father, John Moultrie, was a Scottish immigrant and physician. Not much is known of his mother, Lucretia Cooper. Moultrie had a comfortable middle-class upbringing. He married into his wealth when he wed Damaris Elizabeth de St. Julien. They had an indigo and rice plantation worked by two hundred enslaved people. The couple produced three children; one died in childbirth, a daughter died at age thirteen, and a son served with Moultrie in the army.

Damaris died in 1776. Moultrie remarried, but both his second wife and the surviving son from his first marriage died before him.

Moultrie served in the Provincial Assembly of South Carolina from 1752 to 1762. He was active in the militia and served in the Cherokee War of 1760 to 1761. He was given command of the 2nd Regiment of the South Carolina militia, formed in 1775, as a colonel. He designed the militia flag that became the basis for the current flag of the state of South Carolina. He served in the Battle of Sullivan's Island (1776) and the battles of Beaufort (1779) and Stono Ferry (1779). He also participated in the sieges of Savannah (1779) and Charles Town (1780). His highest rank was major general.

After the revolution, he was twice elected governor of South Carolina. He first served as lieutenant governor from 1784 to 1785 and was then governor from 1785 through 1787. He served in the state senate after his first term and was reelected governor for the 1792-to-1794 term. Moultrie published his memoirs of the revolution in 1802. He died on September 27, 1805, and is buried behind the visitor center at Fort Moultrie on Sullivan's Island.

It was a life of military and political accomplishment filled with personal tragedy. (He also lost a brother serving with him in the defense of Charles Town in 1780.) His *Memoirs of the American Revolution* is over eight hundred pages long and covers two volumes. One would think that a memoir of that length would be full of private insight, detailed analyses, and perhaps criticisms and self-aggrandizement. One would be wrong. The first one hundred pages or so of volume 1 are largely composed of the journals of the Provincial Congress of South Carolina. A significant percentage of the entire two-volume set is either reprinted official proceedings or personal correspondence, with some commentary provided, usually facts. One would think this style and approach would be ineffective in letting the reader see who the man was. However, the memoirs had the opposite effect on me. William Moultrie is revealed by what he says, but even more so by what he doesn't say.

In the preface to his memoirs, Moultrie says he was compelled to write after "having read several other accounts on the subject, and found them very deficient." His goal was to provide "plain detail of the facts." He notes to the reader that "In the course of this reading, it will be found how ignorant we were in the art of war, at the commencement of our revolution." He immediately comes across as direct, opinionated, and humble.

His recounting of events is very matter-of-fact and professional, but he couldn't help himself twice in volume 1 when referring to a certain loyalist:

"Scoffol was a Col. of Militia, a man of some influence in the back country, but a stupid, ignorant, blockhead." (Moultrie, 1802, vol. 1, 109)

"The Scopholites were some of the tories who were led by one Col. Scophol, Col. of militia, an illiterate, stupid, noisy blockhead." (vol. 1, 203)

Both of these observations were in footnotes, as clearly Moultrie didn't want to be that opinionated in the body of his work itself. One wonders what provoked these references, but I appreciated Moultrie's unexpected candor.

Moultrie recounts the events leading up to the June 28 battle, especially his interactions with Charles Lee, but he includes surprisingly little on the day itself: "At the time it was general opinion, especially among the sailors, that two frigates would be a sufficient force to knock the town about our ears: notwithstanding our batteries with heavy cannon; but in a few weeks' time (June 28) experience taught us, that frigates would make no impression upon our palmetto batteries" (vol. 1, 139–40).

On Lee's bridge: "…all his letters to me show how anxious he was at not having a bridge for retreat; for my part, I never was uneasy on not having a bridge because I never imagined that the enemy could force me to that necessity. I always considered myself as able to defend that post against the enemy" (vol. 1, 142).

On Lee's visit during the battle: "Several of the officers, as well as myself, were smoking our pipes and giving orders at the time of action; but laid them down when Gen. Lee came into the fort." (vol. 1, 176)

On the weather: "It may be easily conceived what heat and thirst man must feel in this climate, to be upon a platform on the 28th of June, amidst 20 or 30 heavy pieces of cannon, in one continual blaze and roar; and clouds of smoke curling over our heads for hours together; it was an honorable situation, but a very unpleasant one" (vol. 1, 179).

And his personal health, but only as a footnote: "I had the gout before and at the time of action, on the 28th of June" (vol. 1, 173).

Moultrie jumps out of these pages as direct, opinionated, and humble again but also confident, competent, and honorable. He does not expound on the significance of the victory or the role he played in it. After the battle, he makes no reference to his promotion to general or the renaming of the fort in his honor. One gets the sense that it would be anathema to him to be seen as overpromoting his own legacy.

The defining passage to me on who Moultrie was is contained in volume 2 (166–171). Charles Town has fallen, and Moultrie is on parole. An old English friend, a Lord Montague, writes him with an offer. Montague has been assigned the command of British troops in Jamaica and wants Moultrie to go with him. He posits that Moultrie has done his duty, and he should let "younger hands" take over if "the contest" persists: "You now have a fair opening of quitting that service, with honor and reputation to yourself, by going to Jamaica with me. The world will readily attribute it to the known friendship that has subsisted between us: and by quitting this country for a short time, you would avoid any disagreeable conversations, and might return at leisure to take possession of your estates for yourself and your family." He then offers to hand over his command in Jamaica and serve under Moultrie. The following is an excerpt from Moultrie's response:

I thank you for your wish to promote my advantage, but I am much surprised at your proposition: I flattered myself that I stood in a more favorable light with you but I differ widely with you, in thinking I have discharged my duty to my country, while it is still deluged with blood and over-run with British troops, who exercise the most savage cruelties. When I entered this contest, I did it with the most mature deliberation, and with a determined resolution to risque my life and fortune in the cause...I am sorry you should imagine I have so little regard for my reputation as to listen to such dishonorable proposals...You say, by quitting this country for a short time I might avoid disagreeable conversations, and might return at my leisure and take possession of my estates for myself and family; but you forgot to tell me how I am to get rid of the feelings of an injured honest heart, and where to hide myself from myself: could I be guilty of so much baseness I should hate myself and shun mankind...The repossessing of my estates; the offer of command of your regiment, and the honor you propose of serving under me, are paltry considerations to the loss of my reputation.

Moultrie then tells Montague to propose instead the withdrawal of all British troops from the American continent. He does not end his response with the typical overly flowery close of the times, but rather this: "Think better of me. WM Moultrie."

Who was the real William Moultrie? Moultrie's memoirs depict a great American soldier, statesman, and patriot. His core character traits were competence, confidence, humility, directness, decisiveness, and honor. Like his two favorites, Marion and Jasper, and his colleague in the defense of Sullivan's Island, Danger Thomson, he was a stolid South Carolinian, who cared more about truth, honor, and getting the job done than he did about politics and self-promotion. The only comprehensive biography done on William Moultrie was published in 2013. *Crescent Moon over Carolina*, by C. L. Bragg, is excellent, and I highly recommend it.

MOULTRIE GRAVESITE
Behind the Visitor Center at Fort Moultrie
Sullivan's Island, SC
Source: Photo by author

CHAPTER 6:
THE LOST LEGACY

If the events described here had occurred in New York or New England in 1776, I don't believe the descriptor "unsung" would be applicable. Our national narrative would include the events and the players along with the likes of Bunker Hill and Patrick Henry. It is not just that this story is "lesser" known. This story is not known.

In *The West Point Atlas of American Wars, Volume I 1689–1980* (a "definitive history of American combat"), this is the reference to the Battle of Sullivan's Island: "The initial British offensive in 1776 was in the Carolinas, where Maj. Gen. Sir Henry Clinton's attempt to seize Charleston was severely repulsed" (Esposito, 1995, Map 5).

That's it. Attention, details, and maps all then revert to what was happening in the north. More recently, Pulitzer Prize winner David McCullough's book *1776* had this to say: "An attack on Fort Sullivan at Charleston in June had been such a humiliating defeat for the British that the campaign had to be abandoned, and largely because Clinton had been too cautious" (McCullough, 2005, 165).

That's it. It's there only because of a long discourse on Clinton, who features prominently in the book because, well, he served the British in the north. The victory is assumed to be due to British failures rather than courageous patriotic defense. Our hero, William Moultrie, is not mentioned or referred to in three hundred pages...of a book entitled *1776*! Worse, in *National Geographics Who's Who in American History*, there is no entry for William Moultrie. Charles Lee has an entry, which adds insult to injury.

What are the possible reasons for all this?

1. The events and the battle really weren't that significant. Charles Town fell anyway in 1780, so what's the big deal?

The events and the battle were extremely significant. First, the underdog victory showed incredible resolve and was an inspiration to the emerging nation. The factors that led to victory were almost unbelievable. These included (1) the diversion of the British fleet to Charles Town after Moores Creek Bridge, (2) the faulty British intelligence on the depth of Breach Inlet at low tide, (3) the lack of adequate planning for the army assault on Clinton's part, (4) the un-coordinated naval assault and lack of communication between Parker and

Clinton, (5) the unwavering confidence of William Moultrie in facing down a vastly superior foe and his refusal to abandon his post, and (6) the serendipitous use of palmetto logs in fort construction. The images of victory, including a pantless Peter Parker and a fire plume in the shape of a palmetto, should be the stuff of American legend. The victory was a big deal because Charles Town was free of British control for four years, giving George Washington and the Continental Army the chance to mature without the threat of a southern front. The fall of Charles Town in 1780 is considered the worst defeat of the American Revolution. What if the British had been there in 1776? The strong loyalist and Tory factions would have had a solid base, and the neutral elements of the population would likely be more inclined to go with the perceived winners. The patriots would certainly have put up a fight, but it is likely the British would have had much less difficulty moving up through the Carolinas than they experienced in 1780–81. The revolution was new and risky in 1776. It was much better established and real by 1780.

2. Was it really such an underdog victory? American forces in the area exceeded six thousand men.

It is true that patriot forces in the Charles Town area far exceeded those engaged in the actual fighting on June 28, 1776. However, if the British fleet had reduced the fort on Sullivan's Island, the town of Charles Town would have been vulnerable to direct attack. It is questionable how long the defenders would have held out if the city had been victim to widespread carnage.

The redcoats would also likely have attacked near Haddrell's Point. Would the disjointed combination of patriot militias have stood up to the threat? Would other heroes have emerged? We will never know. What we do know for sure is what happened on June 28, and that alone is worthy of legend status.

3. These events occurred in South Carolina, and no one really paid attention.

Of course, this is an overstatement. But this statement is largely true, I think. New England dominated the news cycle and the patriot press during the revolution. After the Civil War, publishing houses were largely in the North, and any publication glorifying Southern arms, especially in South Carolina, was unlikely to see the light of day. It has only been in the last thirty to forty years that South Carolina's contributions to winning American independence have been written about extensively, and these writings primarily cover 1780 to 1781. During that time, over two hundred battles, skirmishes, and firefights were fought throughout the colony. While it is a reach to argue that the war was won in South Carolina, it is absolutely not a reach to state that, but for South Carolina, the war could have easily been lost. This contribution is not taught in northern schools. In 1960 in Minnesota, I remember watching *The Swamp Fox* on Disney and thinking, "What? The revolution was fought in swamps?" When Mel Gibson's movie *The Patriot* came out in 2000, there was still a similar reaction by many, many Americans.

CONCLUSION

The story of the Battle of Sullivan's Island certainly belongs to all South Carolinians as the basis for the state flag and the state motto: The Palmetto State. But the Battle of Sullivan's Island also belongs to all Americans, as it was a pivotal victory in the early days of our struggle for independence. By preventing the British from establishing a foothold in the southern colonies in 1776, Colonel Moultrie and his previously untested militia bought valuable time for establishing a defense in the Carolinas and for building the Continental Army in the north. The fall of Charleston in 1780 was deemed the biggest defeat of the Revolutionary War. A defeat in 1776 could have been fatal.

William Moultrie is continually underrated as a military leader. He was deemed too easy on his men and too friendly with them. He wasn't an "I'm following orders" guy either. He had a strong sense of purpose, though, and an uncanny level of confidence. He showed up when it mattered. No one ever questioned his competence as a leader in battle. He was not a grandstander or a promotion seeker. He got the job done when it needed to get done. One senses in reading his memoirs, though, that, perhaps, twenty-five years after the fact, he did want to place his and South Carolina's stake in the ground for major contributions that were even then being ignored. Thank goodness he did. He was a very competent military man but even more of a true patriot. He was a great American.

The 250th anniversary of the Battle of Sullivan's Island will occur on June 28, 2026. William Moultrie deserves a proper legacy for his accomplishments in our nation's history. The Battle of Sullivan's Island needs to be taught as a fascinating victory, for sure, but also as a very strategic one. It's time to get the word out on a much broader scale. That goal has been my only intent with this publication.

Acknowledgments

I wish to acknowledge the National Park Service rangers, staff, and volunteers who work tirelessly at Fort Moultrie. They research, interpret, and promote the rich legacy of this unique location in American history. They are ably supported by the Friends of Charleston National Parks, the official philanthropic partner of Fort Moultrie, Fort Sumter, and the Charles Pinckney historical site. I have strived to make the events I describe and the facts I relate true to historical sources. Any errors are mine alone. The opinions I express are also mine alone and do not necessarily reflect any official National Park Service position.

Sources

Major References

Bearss, Edwin C. L. *The Battle of Sullivan's Island and the Capture of Fort Moultrie*. Washington, DC: National Park Service, 1968.

Bragg, C. L. *Crescent Moon Over Carolina; William Moultrie and American Liberty*. United States: University of South Carolina Press, 2013.

Moultrie, William. *Memoirs of the American Revolution, So Far as It Related to the States of North and South Carolina, and Georgia,* United States: D. Longworth, 1802.

Russell, David Lee. *Victory on Sullivan's Island: The British Cape Fear/Charles Town Expedition of 1776*. United States: Infinity Publishing, 2002.

Other Highly Recommended Reading

Buchanan, John. *The Road to Guilford Courthouse: The American Revolution in the Carolinas*. United Kingdom: Turner Publishing Company, 1999.

Oller, John. *The Swamp Fox: How Francis Marion Saved the* American *Revolution*. United States: De Capo Press, 2016.

Other Cited Sources

Boddie, William Willis. *Traditions of the Swamp Fox*. United States: Reprint Company, 2000.

Esposito, Vincent. *The West Point Atlas of American Wars: Volume 1, 1689–1900*. United States: Henry Holt & Company. 1995 (revised and updated version of the original, published in 1959).

McCullough, David. *1776*. United States: Thorndike Press, 2005.

Thompson, J. M., W. R. Gray and K. M. Kostyal. *Who's Who in American History: Leaders, Visionaries, and Icons Who Shaped Our Nation*, United States: National Geographic Press, 2017

About the Author

Norm Rickeman is a retired business consultant who now resides on Sullivan's Island. A lifetime history nut, he began volunteering for the National Park Service at Fort Moultrie in 2021. A native Minnesotan, he was familiar with Francis Marion and Osceola, who figure prominently with Fort Moultrie history, but he had never heard of William Moultrie or the Battle of Sullivan's Island. The more he learned and read, the more fascinated he became. The story also resonated with the hundreds of visitors he engaged at Fort Moultrie from all over the country and world. Most of these visitors had little or no knowledge of the events of June 28, 1776. He began speaking on the subject in 2024 with his *Unsung: William Moultrie and the Battle of Sullivan's Island* talk. This publication is a companion piece to that presentation. Norm has a mathematics and economics degree from the University of Minnesota and an MBA from the University of Chicago.

Milton Keynes UK
Ingram Content Group UK Ltd.
UKHW020217151124
451096UK00020B/244

9 798822 961234